Dear Parent:
Your child's love of

Every child learns to read in a ～～～～ own
speed. Some go back and fort～～～ad
favorite books again and again. ～～～ read through each level in
order. You can help your young reader improve and become more
confident by encouraging his or her own interests and abilities. From
books your child reads with you to the first books he or she reads
alone, there are I Can Read Books for every stage of reading:

SHARED READING
Basic language, word repetition, and whimsical illustrations,
ideal for sharing with your emergent reader

BEGINNING READING
Short sentences, familiar words, and simple concepts
for children eager to read on their own

READING WITH HELP
Engaging stories, longer sentences, and language play
for developing readers

READING ALONE
Complex plots, challenging vocabulary, and high-interest topics
for the independent reader

ADVANCED READING
Short paragraphs, chapters, and exciting themes
for the perfect bridge to chapter books

I Can Read Books have introduced children to the joy of reading
since 1957. Featuring award-winning authors and illustrators and a
fabulous cast of beloved characters, I Can Read Books set the
standard for beginning readers.

A lifetime of discovery begins with the magical words "I Can Read!"

Visit www.icanread.com for information
on enriching your child's reading experience.

barre

 ponies

 bottles

 pony

 feet

 ribbons

 flowers

 toe shoes

 hairbrush

 tutu

 piano

 tutus

Tutus and Toe Shoes

by *Ruth Benjamin*
illustrated by *Lyn Fletcher*

HarperCollins*Publishers*

Twinkle Twirl's dance school

was about to open.

She had everything ready.

The  waited outside.

"Welcome to dance

school!" called Twinkle Twirl.

First, Twinkle Twirl taught

the  how to dress.

"Ballerinas wear a

and  , and

in their hair.

You should pack a dance

bag with your clothes,

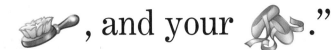 , and your ."

Twinkle Twirl told the

to bring  of water.

"Dancing is hard work!"

she told them.

"Spinning in your

will make you thirsty!"

Next, Twinkle Twirl taught

the  the five positions.

They stretched at the ____ .

They pointed their toes.

They waved their arms.

They bent to touch

their ____ .

Soon it was time

for the  to dance.

Two by two,

they moved across the floor.

They held hands

and skipped their 🩰 .

Their 🌸 bounced

and their 🎀 twirled.

Twinkle Twirl showed the

 how to leap.

She showed them how

to be light on their  .

Her  flew with her.

"Now each  will try

a leap," said Twinkle Twirl.

Pinkie Pie was afraid

to leap across the floor.

She hid behind the  .

Then she tripped

on her laces.

Oops! She fell to the floor.

"What happened?" said
Cheerilee.

"I was scared to try a leap,"
said Pinkie Pie.

"Sometimes teamwork can
help!" said Rainbow Dash.

Pinkie Pie fixed her .

She was ready to try.

The  showed

Pinkie Pie what to do.

"Bend your knees and lift

your arms," said Cheerilee.

"Now point your

and jump!" said Scootaloo.

"You can do it!" they said.

Pinkie Pie leaped.

The  cheered.

"Hooray!" said Twinkle Twirl.

Rainbow Dash gave

Pinkie Pie .

"I could not have done it

without you," said Pinkie Pie.

"Friends are the best part

of dance school!"

Pinkie Pie took a bow.

"I can't wait to come back!"

she said.